Hurricane Henry

GB

This book is dedicated to Potcake Place K9 Rescue and all the great work they do.
www.potcakeplace.com

We're here, we're here Molly shouted at the top of her voice. Molly was sooooo excited to be here on Sunshine Island, it felt like she had been waiting forever.

Now, this holiday was special but Molly did not know just how special it was going to be.

68822

Then she saw it!!! THE PUPPY HOTEL, Molly was confused, was this a hotel where puppies lived? Yes it was, and even better you could take the puppies for a walk everyday!!!

Molly burst through the doors and all she saw was puppies, puppies everywhere!!!!

Puppy Hotel

Oh Mummy, how can I choose, Molly screamed in the most excited voice.

Then she heard it....an odd little noise..... she listened closely, it could only be described as a bark followed by a....whistle?

Molly followed the noise and there he was, there was little Henry stuck in the corner just waiting to be heard.

Molly had decided it was going to be Henry OR had Henry decided it was going to be Molly.

The next few days were so special, Molly and Henry were already best friends.

Their favourite place was the beach. They went there every day.

They ran up and down the white sands, they played in the water, they sat on the beach while Molly told Henry stories of the big city she lived in and the naughty cat next door.

Morning arrived and Molly sprang out of bed, time for Henry's walk she beamed. But something wasn't right, the sky was grey, and there was a howling sound that was wrapping itself around the building .

It scared her, then she thought of Henry!

MUMMY we need to get Henry... but they couldn't, this was a hurricane and they were not allowed to leave until it stopped.
Mummy assured Molly that Henry would be safe in his Puppy Hotel.
If only Mummy knew that wasn't the case.

Poor Henry was very scared, it was dark and loud. Henry had never heard or seen a hurricane before, and then suddenly, a loud bang!

He took his paws from his eyes and saw that the door of the Puppy Hotel had blown away, he didnt know what to do, so he ran and ran into the darkness.

He just knew he needed to find his best friend and everything would be ok.

Henry wondered where Molly would be, then it came to him.
Molly would be on the beach, it was their favorite place!

When Henry got to the beach everything had changed.
Where did the sand go? Why was the water so angry? Where was Molly!!!

HE WAS ALONE and lost in the dark. Poor Henry.

The Hurricane had stopped and Molly and her mummy ran as fast as they could to the Puppy Hotel but Henry wasn't there.

Brave Molly looked at her Mummy and said, I know where he will be, he will be at the beach, it's our favorite place Mummy.

Henry MUST be there!!!

They got to the beach but there was no Henry. Molly couldn't be brave any more and she started to cry, shouting for Henry through her tears.

Meanwhile Henry opened his eyes and realized he was still all alone. He started to bark his unique bark over and over again, whistling into the sunny day.

Molly jumped to her feet, she would know that whistle anywhere.She ran as fast as she could towards the whistle shouting "Henry Henry".

Henry jumped to his feet and ran towards the shouting.

They were so happy to be back together again.

They cried tears of happiness as they rolled around in the sand. Henry's unique whistle had saved them both.

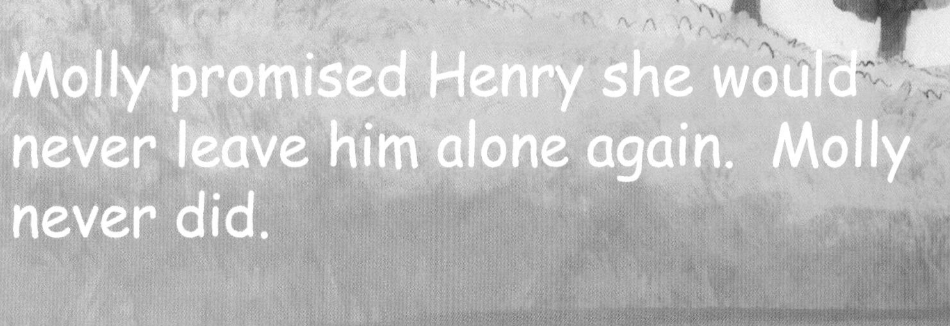

Molly promised Henry she would never leave him alone again. Molly never did.

Henry went to live with Molly and her family in New York where their adventures were just beginning!!!

I told you it was a very special holiday!!!!

For all the people of ‘Potcake Place’. Thank you for your hard work in keeping every single puppy happy and healthy for that one special friend who is already on their way toward Sunshine Island.

please donate here ……www.potcakeplace.com

Printed in Great Britain
by Amazon